GOPHER DRAWS CONCLUSIONS

Virginia Scribner

illustrated by Janet Wilson

VIKING

VIKING
Published by the Penguin Group
Penguin Books USA Inc., 375 Hudson Street, New York,
New York 10014, U.S.A.
Penguin Books Ltd, 27 Wrights Lane, London W8 5TZ, England
Penguin Books Australia Ltd, Ringwood, Victoria, Australia
Penguin Books Canada Ltd, 10 Alcorn Avenue, Toronto, Ontario,
Canada M4V 3B2
Penguin Books (N.Z.) Ltd, 182–190 Wairau Road, Auckland 10,
New Zealand

Penguin Books Ltd, Registered Offices: Harmondsworth,
Middlesex, England

First published in 1994 by Viking, a division of Penguin Books USA Inc.

1   3   5   7   9   10   8   6   4   2

LIBRARY OF CONGRESS CATALOGING-IN-PUBLICATION DATA
Scribner, Virginia.
Gopher draws conclusions / by Virginia Scribner ;
illustrated by Janet Wilson.   p.   cm.
Summary: When Kevin wins an art contest using a drawing that
Gopher had given him, Gopher must make a difficult choice between
revenge and saving their friendship.
ISBN 0-670-85660-6
[1. Friendship—Fiction.   2. Revenge—Fiction.]
I. Wilson, Janet, ill.   II. Title.
PZ7.S43615G1   1994   [Fic]—dc20   94-20286   CIP   AC

Printed in U.S.A.
Set in Bookman

To my husband, Elie

I would like to thank Virginia Smith,
dear friend for twenty-four years,
for her invaluable contributions to this book.
—V.S.

Contents

The Police Arrive

Gopher was still in his pajamas, brushing his teeth, when he heard the doorbell ring. That's strange, he thought. Who would be coming to the house this early on a Saturday morning?

His father answered the door. "Yes?" It was a deep man's voice that spoke next. After a moment Gopher's father called up the stairs. "Oh, Matthew, could you come here right away?"

When Gopher's father said "Matthew," he meant Gopher. Like all grown-ups he refused to call his son by his nickname. "Gopher" came from the kids adding an -er to his last name, Goff.

"It's not that we *suspect* your son, you understand," the deep voice continued.

Gopher put down his toothbrush. Suspect your son? What was the man talking about?

"Matthew, are you coming?"

"Dad, I'm not dressed. Just a minute, okay?"

"Okay, but please hurry."

Gopher quickly threw off his pajamas. He grabbed for his underpants and blue jeans. He found a T-shirt. Gee. What was happening? He shoved his bare feet into his sneakers and rushed out of the room.

From the top of the stairs he could see his father talking to a police officer. The man was wearing a slightly-too-tight blue uniform. He had a clipboard with him. He was writing something down.

"Matthew," his father said when he joined them, "this officer says Jason Bosworth's skateboard was stolen yesterday afternoon. He's wondering if you know anything about it?"

Jason Bosworth was a seventh grader who lived a few doors away. Gopher, who was in fifth grade, didn't have anything to do with him. Why would this man think he did?

"Don't get me wrong," said the officer. "We don't think *you* did it. We just wonder if you've noticed anything strange going on. You're one of the closest neighbors." As the man spoke Gopher studied his reddish, shiny-clean face. It gave a clear message: Don't Mess with Me. Gopher had no intention of doing anything of the kind.

"I don't know anything about it," Gopher answered truthfully. "I hardly ever see Jason. I didn't even know he *had* a skateboard."

Gopher glanced at the officer's gun. He could only see the corner of its black handle. The rest of the weapon was hidden in a shiny leather holster. Steel bullets, tightly held in loops, circled the man's thick waist.

"Officer, tell me something." Gopher's father, having heard Gopher's answer, seemed a little more relaxed. "Isn't it rather unusual to go house to house for a *skate-board?*"

"Well, it is, sir." The blue-uniformed officer sure was polite, Gopher thought, for someone so scary-looking. "It's just that we've had eight skateboards stolen this month. We have no idea what's going on. We think maybe somebody's stealing them to sell. Probably for drugs."

Gopher's father shook his head in disgust. Gopher waited for him to say, "Well, in England . . . " but he didn't.

"Okay. Thanks, anyway." The huge officer put his pen back in his shirt pocket. Then, from what appeared to be habit, he patted his gun. "By the way"—he was speaking to Gopher—"do *you* have a skateboard?"

Gopher admitted that he had. It was a Tony Hawk. His dad had gotten it for him in San Diego on one of his many business trips. Skateboarding was one of Gopher's favorite activities.

"Well, you'd better keep it locked up." The

officer casually looked past Gopher into the room behind him. "I'd even recommend coming down to the station and having it engraved with your name. Thieves can't sell a well-marked skateboard. Sometimes we find them in the dump."

"Isn't it a shame, these young people, making such a botch of it?" Gopher could tell his dad was trying hard to please.

The officer sighed in agreement and began scanning the area behind Gopher's dad. "Okay, then." He waved cheerfully, as if he hadn't been sneaking looks at the interior of the Goff house. He patted his gun again. "If you see anything, you'll call headquarters?" Gopher's dad said of course, and the officer left.

Gopher let out a huge breath. He knew he wasn't in any kind of trouble. Still, having a big gun-carrying police officer sneaking looks around your house was pretty nerve-racking.

Wait until he told Kevin!

A Good Day Ahead

"Well, how was that for a little excitement? Before breakfast, yet?" Gopher's father rubbed his hands together. He had a way of doing that whenever he was nervous. He and Gopher were walking into the kitchen. Gopher's mother was reading the paper.

"What was that about?" she asked, casually looking up.

"Oh, just the police, wondering if our son was a thief."

She crinkled her face into a grin. "I hope you said he *wasn't*."

His father grunted and handed Gopher a thick slice of homemade bread on a blue plate. "Mom obviously doesn't consider it a very serious matter," he said, half-smiling.

His mother lowered her paper to look at them. "You guys want to go for a hot air balloon ride this afternoon?" She showed them the page she was reading. It featured a huge picture of a hot air balloon drifting through the sky. "It says here they're having rides up at the university. We don't get this chance every day, here in Rhode Island."

"Not me." Gopher's father shuddered. "Not in a hundred years!"

She turned to Gopher. "Well, how about you? You could ask Kevin. We'll go after lunch. It says here it's supposed to be sunny all day."

"You're thinking of taking our child . . ." Gopher's father coughed several times. Apparently he had swallowed something the wrong way. ". . . in one of *those* contraptions?"

"Really, Howard."

"Gee, that would be great, Mom. I'll call Kevin as soon as I finish breakfast." Boy, he could hardly believe his good luck. A hot air balloon ride! He'd always wanted to go on one of those things!

He took a bite of the delicious bread. Somebody—he guessed his father—had slathered it with warm butter and raspberry jam, his favorite combination.

"Mmmm," said his mother, turning to another section of the paper.

That was exactly what Gopher was thinking. She wasn't eating though, so he wondered what she was *mmmming* about.

As if she'd read his mind, she folded the paper. "Here's something you might find interesting."

She handed him *The Kids' Page,* a special section of the paper with kids' features and puzzles and stuff. She had folded it to highlight a square with about six squiggly lines in it. Gopher continued eating while he read.

"They're having a contest," he said. "You're

supposed to make a picture using these squiggles."

"Now, *that's* a good idea," said Gopher's father.

He was referring to the fact that Gopher was good in art. He'd even won the Christmas art contest at school. The principal had displayed his painting of Santa brushing down Rudolph outside his office until a few days after Valentine's Day. Now it was in a plastic frame up in Gopher's room.

A dime-sized dab of butter dripped onto the newspaper, just missing the contest entry blank. He read some more. "And it says the best one wins twenty-five dollars!"

His mother smiled. "I was wondering when you'd notice that."

Gopher studied the squiggles again, harder this time. Twenty-five dollars would allow him to buy that used airbrush at Mr. Mahoney's store. He'd seen a guy using one last summer at the beach. With his airbrush he'd painted people's names or flowers or whatever they'd asked for. Some people had wanted the slogan "Biggest Little State in the Union" with pictures of boats and seagulls and the whole bit. In about three minutes the man had transformed a three-dollar plain T-shirt into a fifteen-dollar decorated one.

Wow! The police officer, a hot air balloon ride, and now a chance to win twenty-five dollars! Gopher could tell, this was going to be a lucky day. And then, the phone rang.

Kevin Gets
Another Pet!

The call was from Kevin. "We'll be over in fifteen minutes. Dad's taking us to the pond this morning. Get worms. Bye."

"Wait—" That Kevin! He'd hung up before Gopher had a chance to tell him about the police officer or even the hot air balloon ride.

Everyone got busy. Gopher's dad said he'd get out the fishing gear. His mother started to pack a lunch. Gopher ran to the leaf pile behind the garage. "Here's a good one." He picked up a slippery worm about the size of a skinny McDonald's french fry. He put the worm in a rusty coffee can half full of dirt.

Honnnnnnk! The Gordons' red pickup

truck pulled into the driveway. Gopher knew it was Kevin, not Mr. Gordon, honking the horn. "C'mon, c'mon, we gotta get going." That was Kevin, too.

Gopher's father rushed up carrying two bulky orange life jackets. "Now, I want you both to wear these *all* the time, even when you're on the shore."

Gopher's mom came out of the house with a paper bag in her hand. "Here's your lunch. Be back by two, so we can go on that hot air balloon ride. You're coming with us, aren't you, Kevin?"

Kevin's eyes went wide. "We're going on a hot air balloon ride?" He socked Gopher. "You never tell me anything!"

When they arrived at the pond, Mr. Gordon helped them untie the boat and get it into the water. "I'll be back around one-thirty," he said, "unless it rains." He scanned the darkening sky. "You'd better stay on this side of the pond today. Just in case."

The boys agreed and waved good-bye.

They rowed to a good spot. Gopher dug into the can of worms. First he told Kevin about the police officer and all those stolen skateboards. Then he changed the subject. "Maybe I'll be able to buy that airbrush at Mr. Mahoney's soon." He threw his loaded hook into the water.

"Yeah, how come?" Kevin was intently watching the red-and-white plastic bobber on his line. It bounced merrily on each little ripple of water. Even *it* was having a good time.

"Well, there's a contest in the paper." Gopher told about the six squiggly lines.

Then Kevin had his own news. "I have a new pet," he said. Gopher shook his head in disbelief. Kevin's family already had two dogs (Andy and Randy), a cat (Candy), and a bird (Sandy). Kevin sure was lucky to have all those pets. Gopher didn't even have one.

"Yeah, I was out near the brook with Randy and Andy when all of a sudden they

started barking like crazy. When I got closer, what do you think I saw?"

"A frog?" Gopher pulled in his fishing line. The hook was bare.

"No, not a frog." Kevin grinned from ear to ear. "A garter snake."

"Big deal." Gopher pretended to be unimpressed. It wasn't fair. How come Kevin got to have so many pets? "Is your mom going to let you keep it *in the house?*" He thought even Mrs. Gordon must have her limits.

But it seemed not. "Oh, yeah. In fact, she said she'd like having a snake."

"She'd *like* having a snake?"

They fished, wordlessly, for a couple of minutes. "Where are you going to keep it?" Gopher asked eventually. "Seems to me Randy or Andy, or even Candy, would like to eat it."

"No problem. I already made him a neat cage."

Kevin's bobber plunged into the water. He

stopped talking to pay attention. "False alarm," he said, pulling up the bare hook.

"What are you going to name it?" asked Gopher, going back to the snake. "You've just about used up all the -*andy* names."

Kevin was wriggling a squishy pinky tan worm onto his hook. "Yeah, I know. We went through the alphabet and thought of Dandy, and Mandy, and Handy. We didn't like any of those, so I said we might as well name him Gartner." He wiped his dirty hands on his pants. "Kind of a combination of partner and garter, you know."

Gopher considered. It seemed too bad to ruin the design of the pet names—Andy, Randy, Candy, and Sandy—with Gartner! It just didn't fit. He went through the alphabet himself. *A* they had already taken with Andy. *B?*

Then he thought of it. "How about Bandy?"

"Bandy?"

"Sure. You know how snakes have their colors sort of in bands up and down their bodies? Bandy would be for those bands, get it?"

"Hey, that's a great name!"

Gopher was glad he was able to help Kevin come up with a good name. But it made him a little sad that he only got to *name* pets, he never got to own one. His mother was "allergic" to dust. Not in the way most people were—their bodies reacted. No, in her case, it wasn't her body. It was *her.* Although she didn't get hyper about most stuff, for dust she made an exception.

But what about a snake? Nobody could say a snake was dusty. *Maybe* she'd let him have one.

"Hey, I think it's a real bite this time," shouted Kevin from his end of the boat.

Just then the first rumble of thunder sounded from across the pond.

Rained Out

"Oh, no!" cried Kevin. "Just when we were beginning to get bites!" He twisted his mouth into an S shape. Whenever things didn't go his way, Kevin's mouth always did this special trick.

Several drops of rain gently splattered onto the pond. If the rain stayed at this level, maybe they could continue fishing. Gopher had always heard that fishing was best in the rain. Now he might have a chance to find out.

There was a clap of thunder. The rain got harder. "We're done for," wailed Kevin. "We might as well get back."

Soon the whole sky opened up, and the rain came down in buckets. They were soaked to the skin by the time Mr. Gordon arrived. He ran out of the truck, covering his head with a newspaper. Gopher noticed the picture of the hot air balloon. Mr. Gordon was covering his head with the same newspaper that said what a sunny day it was supposed to be! "Well, that was a short fishing trip," he called to the boys.

The three of them tied the boat onto the truck. "Don't feel bad," said Mr. Gordon. "Maybe we'll go have lunch at McDonald's. Matt, you want to come, too?"

Even lunch at McDonald's wasn't enough to cheer Kevin up. He mumbled something about how it *always* rains in Rhode Island, especially on the weekends. One thing about Kevin, he was either very happy or very sad, hardly ever in the middle.

Mr. Gordon started up the truck and they were off. Now he was saying that Kevin should clean up the workroom he'd left in such a mess last night from making the snake's cage. Gopher knew that would put Kevin in an even worse mood.

"You wanna come over?" Kevin asked. "It shouldn't take too long to clean the workroom. Then we could mess around with Bandy and stuff."

Gopher almost accepted, but then he remembered the squiggly lines contest. He loved projects like that. He told Kevin his plan.

"Hey, Dad, can I see that paper?" Reaching behind the seat, Kevin grabbed the soggy paper. He turned to *The Kids' Page*. "I think I'll enter too," he announced.

"Ha!" scoffed Gopher. "You don't know how to draw!"

"Yeah? Who says?"

That Kevin couldn't draw was so obvious that Gopher didn't think he needed to give a *reason*. But he thought of one. "Remember what Ms. Connors said about your picture last week?"

"What?" Kevin, as always, wasn't going to admit he was wrong, even (especially) if he was.

"She said, 'Kevin, would you please tell us about your picture?' That's what she always says when she has *no clue* what a kid's picture's about."

"That's not so!" Kevin was getting more and more excited. "After I told her it was two frogs sunbathing on a green lily pad, she said it was very clever. She even laughed."

"I'll say. All it was, was a green blob with one little yellow part and another little red one. You said those were the lady frog's bikini."

Mr. Gordon's lips turned up at that remark, Gopher noticed.

"Yeah? And who made *you* the Drawing Champion of the World?"

"Well, at least I don't make a joke out of every art project." Then Gopher thought of something else. "Like your diorama of a famous landmark. You were the one who said your Mount Rushmore looked like four rats with a skin condition."

"So?" Kevin's mouth was so curled that

the S was closer to an 8. He made a fist and shoved it near Gopher's face.

"Boys, boys," said Mr. Gordon. "Calm down."

Luckily they were just pulling into Gopher's driveway. "Why don't you just go home and draw your dumb picture?" Kevin shouted as Gopher struggled to open the door. "And I hope you *don't* win the crummy contest, so there!"

Now Gopher's day was completely turned around. It had started out being a sunny day of fishing with his best friend. They were even going on a hot air balloon ride. Now it was a dreary, rainy day with his best friend mad at him. No fishing. And no hot air balloon ride, either.

Gopher knew his parents weren't home, so he went to the garage to get the spare key they kept in the bicycle-tire repair can. As he unlocked the door, he remembered it wasn't as bad as it could be. At least he still had the squiggly lines contest.

Trace and Draw

As Gopher entered the kitchen, he noticed it was spotless, as always. He wondered what was in the lunch that he hadn't gotten to eat. He opened the bag. There was a tuna fish sandwich, an apple, some carrot sticks, and two packages of chocolate cupcakes. His mom, Mrs. Junk-Food-Is-Terrible, had bought those!

Obviously one package had been for him and one for Kevin. Now that they were mad at each other, Gopher guessed he'd get to eat both packages himself. He took one out and put the rest of the lunch in the refrigerator.

That day's newspaper was lying on the kitchen table. It was neatly folded with *The*

Kids' Page showing. He picked it up and, carrying his cupcakes, went to his room.

Gopher's room, like the rest of the house, was very tidy. His dad had built a whole bunch of shelves in the back of his large closet. That was where Gopher kept his drawing pads and other supplies.

Gopher sat at his large desk and took a bite of cupcake. He looked hard at the squiggles. This is do-able, he thought.

He remembered a filmstrip he'd seen at school. It was about Arnold Lobel, the writer and illustrator. Mr. Lobel had said he owed his whole career to tracing paper. He explained how he would draw a picture and then redraw the picture, using tracing paper. On the tracing paper he'd leave in the parts he liked and change the parts he didn't like.

Since then, Gopher had started using this technique in his own drawing. He got out a sheet of tracing paper.

He looked and looked at those squiggles.

At first no ideas came to him. It occurred to him that coming up with an idea was a little like fishing. You had to be patient and wait for a bite. But you also had to keep throwing in your line.

Then, still not having a clear idea of what he was going to do, he put the tracing paper on top of the entry blank and began. He extended one of the lines. It seemed to want to make a nose. He made the nose, but then another squiggle was in the wrong place for the rest of the face. He erased his line and tried again.

He worked like that for maybe an hour. Finally he had all six squiggles as part of a picture. It was a robot in the shape of a fierce dinosaur. He had studied dinosaurs in school several times. And he liked robots too. Combining the two ideas was a lucky inspiration.

Once he had the idea down and the original lines in place, the rest was easy. He got so engrossed that he was a little surprised when his father called from downstairs to say they were home.

Gopher got the drawing as good as he could. Then he went to show his parents. "Nice, Matt," said his father. "Very, *very* good," said his mother. Gopher knew she must have really liked it. Otherwise, she would have said it was "fine."

The picture had turned out so good Gopher wanted to show it to somebody else. Too bad Kevin was so mad. He felt a little sorry for those mean words he'd said about Kevin's artwork. So what if Kevin wanted to butt in on his contest? He'd never win anyway.

Maybe he's over it by now, thought Gopher. Kevin didn't usually stay mad all day. And it had stopped raining. Gopher decided he'd go show Kevin the picture— and hope for the best.

Dino-Mighty

As Gopher had hoped, Kevin greeted him as if nothing had happened. Gopher held out the dinosaur-robot drawing. "Wanna see?"

Kevin took the paper and held it at arm's length. His whole face lit up. "Wow, this is fan-tas-tic!" Gopher giggled. When Kevin liked something, he really liked it. Kevin stared at the picture for several seconds. "You got all *those* lines to make *this* picture?"

"Well, I thought it turned out okay."

Kevin nearly danced out of his skin. " 'Okay'? This is the best picture you ever made! What do you mean, 'okay'? It's dynamite!"

Gopher felt as happy as that red-and-white bobber bouncing about in the ripples of the pond earlier that morning. He was *so glad* Kevin was his best friend! In fact, he was so delighted that he said something he hadn't been planning on. "You want this picture, Kevin? You can have it."

As soon as the words were out, Gopher wished he could take them back. What was he doing? He needed that picture to enter the contest!

But Kevin's response made that impossible. "Wow, thanks!" He grabbed the picture and ordered Gopher to come with him to his room.

Kevin's room was the exact opposite of Gopher's. Every surface, including the floor, the bed, the chair, the dresser, even the tops of the books in his bookshelf, was covered with stuff. Kevin didn't believe in putting anything away. He started rummaging in a messy drawer. After a moment he picked up a bent green thumbtack. He

tacked Gopher's picture onto his closet door. It went over several thicknesses of papers already displayed there.

"Looks mighty good," he said proudly. One would think he himself had drawn it. "Yep. *mighty* good." He turned to Gopher. "Hey, that's an idea. I'm going to call it Dino-Mighty. Get it? It's a dinosaur and it's mighty good and it's dynamite." He stuck out his chest. "See, Goph? I'm not so bad at thinking up names myself."

"Speaking of names . . . " Gopher pointed to a cage about the size of a small television set. "I take it this is where Bandy lives?" The cage was a typical "Kevin project." Some boards were longer than others. There were sizable gaps where the wood didn't come together.

Gopher removed the heavy wooden cover. He reached in and picked up Bandy. The graceful creature curled his smooth, dry body around Gopher's hand. His intelligent eyes scanned the surroundings. Turning his head from side to side, he whisked out a silvery pink tongue.

The two boys played with Bandy awhile, and then Kevin suggested they go skateboarding. Gopher reminded him they'd first have to stop at his house to pick up his skateboard. "No problem," said Kevin. "And let's stop at Mr. Mahoney's, too. I want to see if he still has Fried Clyde. I sure hope so."

Gopher sure hoped so, too.

Mr. Mahoney's Store

After stopping at Gopher's, the two boys walked into Mr. Mahoney's store, each one carrying his own skateboard. "Well, look who's here!" said Mr. Mahoney. He was arranging some fishing lures in the front display case. "Always glad to see my two best helpers! Whatcha been up to, Kevin?"

Gopher was used to Mr. Mahoney giving special attention to Kevin. He figured that was because they were both junk collectors, each in his own way.

Mr. Mahoney's store was crammed with secondhand stuff. You could get anything you wanted there: a tennis racket, a camping lantern, a popcorn popper. Gopher noticed his airbrush was still in the case. Fried Clyde, the skateboard with the monster turtle on the bottom, was still where it belonged, too. Gopher and Kevin guessed the turtle got that name because it looked like it was being fried by a bolt of lightning. Kevin, whose own skateboard was falling apart, had his heart set on owning it.

"I see you still have Fried Clyde," he announced. He put his own skateboard on the floor. "I'm up to thirteen dollars now, plus the ten dollars I have with you on account."

Kevin's account came about because sometimes Mr. Mahoney hired the boys to pick up a truckload with him. They liked that—they got to see all the "new" stuff before anybody else. And he paid them, too. For every trip he'd give them each five dollars' credit to buy anything in the store. Both Gopher's airbrush and Kevin's skateboard cost a lot more than five dollars. So far, they each had ten dollars saved.

Mr. Mahoney reached for the skateboard and took the white price tag between two fingers. "That means you only have thirty-six dollars to go." Smiling, he handed the

skateboard to Kevin. Kevin didn't smile back.

Two thoughts occurred to Gopher. One was, how in the world could Mr. Mahoney do that arithmetic so fast in his head? The other was, it would be a *long* time before Kevin could get thirty-six dollars. He'd been saving for ages just to get thirteen. As for picking up a truckload, that only happened once in a while.

Mr. Mahoney put his hand on Kevin's shoulder. "You know, Kevin, Fried Clyde is the most expensive skateboard I've got. It's a Mike Carroll. Practically brand-new. See the trucks and wheels?— hardly used. If you'd settle for one of these other skateboards, I could let you have it for what you've already saved."

Kevin didn't say anything, only shook his head.

"How long have you been saving, Kevin?"

"Ever since my birthday, and that was almost a year ago."

"I tell you what, Kevin. I'll lower the price

ten dollars. That way all you need is twenty-six dollars more. In fact, let's say twenty-five dollars and it's yours."

Gopher knew that twenty-five dollars might as well be twenty-five *hundred* dollars to Kevin. He watched as his friend lovingly spun the wheels. They made a quiet, soothing whirl. Kevin held the skateboard so the picture on the bottom faced Gopher. "*Augha-aughhhha!*" he said, supplying the sound for the leering turtle with claws outstretched. Then, with a sigh, he gave the skateboard back to Mr. Mahoney.

"Hey, Kev, tell Mr. Mahoney about Bandy."

Kevin's face changed as if someone had zapped a (mild) bolt of lightning through *him*. "I've got a new pet, Mr. Mahoney. It's a garter snake. I keep him in a cage I built myself. I'm calling him Bandy. It's a name Gopher thought of." Gopher's plan had worked: Kevin had completely forgotten about Fried Clyde.

"That's very interesting, Kevin. You know how to take care of him?"

"I think so. Just give him some raw hamburger and some water, right?"

"Live bugs are even better. They provide calcium for his bones."

"Gopher! We gotta go home!" With Kevin everything was an emergency. They'd find some bugs, but couldn't Bandy survive a few hours without his calcium?

"Although if you can't find bugs," added Mr. Mahoney, "worms will do."

Gopher and Kevin started for the door. "Hey, Kev, your skateboard." Gopher pointed to Kevin's old skateboard, which he had forgotten to pick up from the floor. Kevin looked at the object with mild disgust, almost as if he didn't think it was worth bending down for. Then, reluctantly, he stooped down and picked it up.

"Before you go, Kevin, wait." Mr. Mahoney walked to the back. "Someone just brought in . . . yes, here it is." He returned carrying a glass fish tank. "It leaks, so it can't be used for fish anymore, but it might be a good place to keep Bandy if your cage doesn't work out."

"Thanks, Mr. Mahoney, but I'm all set. My cage is terrific. I even put a handle on it so I can take him with me when I go places. I'll bring him down here someday." As they left, Kevin said what Gopher knew he was going to. "Do you mind not going skateboarding today? I have to go home and feed Bandy some bugs!" Then he frowned at the well-used skateboard in his hands. "And who wants to go skateboarding with this junky thing, anyway?"

Even though Gopher had been looking forward to going skateboarding, he told Kevin he didn't mind. You had to do what your friend wanted once in a while. And besides, he knew Kevin was in his sad-funky mood. He always was, after he visited Fried Clyde and realized once again that he'd never have enough money to buy it.

"So," Gopher asked, "where do we look first for bugs?"

Another Chance?

As they continued on their way home, Kevin seemed to be thinking about something. "Uh, Gopher?"

"Yeah?"

"That picture of Dino-Mighty?"

"Yeah?"

"How're you gonna enter the contest if you gave it to me?"

"I don't know." Gopher hoped Kevin was about to say he'd give it back.

"Hmmm, you think you could make another one? Or maybe you could Xerox it?"

"No, the rules say no photocopies," said Gopher. "But maybe I could make another one . . . if I had another entry blank."

The two boys walked farther. After a few

minutes, Kevin stopped and turned to Gopher. "Hey, I know! You can have the blank out of *our* paper. It must be around someplace."

"Great!" Gopher could make a new Dino-Mighty fairly easily. He still had the tracing paper he'd used in his trace-and-draw method. He might be able to win the money for that airbrush after all.

"But, remember, first we've got to feed Bandy."

When they got to Kevin's house, the search for bugs began. They checked the grass near the brook, but there wasn't a grasshopper or a cricket to be found. "Here's where I found Bandy," said Kevin. He pointed to a place near a half-rotten log. "Let's see if he has a brother or sister. You'd like a snake, too, wouldn't you?"

"Of course! Who wouldn't?"

But there were no snakes and no bugs. Giving up, the two boys walked over to get a worm from Gopher's leaf pile behind the garage. "One should be enough," said Kevin. "Snakes don't eat much." They found a worm with no problem and began the walk back. Kevin chuckled. "Talk about a waste of energy. Two kids walk six blocks, round trip, to get one worm."

When they removed the heavy lid to put in the worm, Bandy looked fine, but he hadn't eaten the raw hamburger. "Here, Bandy," said Kevin, "have a nice, juicy worm. Yummmmmm."

After Bandy was fed, Gopher and Kevin started looking for the newspaper. Katie, Kevin's third-grade sister, was sitting at the kitchen table. She was coloring with a bluish purple crayon on what appeared to be newspaper. "Katie," Kevin shouted, "stop!"

Katie glanced up.

"You're coloring on Gopher's entry blank, the one he wanted to send in to the paper!"

Katie shot her older brother a look. "Who gave you that information?" she asked.

"Who gave you that information?" Kevin

mimicked. He reached to grab the paper away. The blunt end of a bluish purple crayon jabbed hard into his hand. He pulled away.

"Mommmm!" Katie yelled. "Kevin's bothering me."

Gopher noticed that Katie's paper wasn't the squiggly lines contest. It was a picture of smiling children running out of a store with packages in their arms. He told Kevin.

Katie went back to coloring. "I happen to be entering the Sensational Spring Sweepstakes. The kid who colors this picture the best wins a six-foot rabbit and five pounds of candy eggs. So, there."

Kevin looked more closely at the picture. "Oh." Changing his tone of voice but not admitting that he'd made a mistake, he continued, "Anyway, have you seen today's paper? Gopher needs it."

Katie faced her brother and pulled back her bangs. "What does it say here?" She was pointing to her forehead.

"Huh? It doesn't say anything."

"That's a relief." She withdrew a peachy pink crayon and resumed coloring. "From the way you're talking, I thought it said 'Lost and Found.'"

"Very funny, Katie, very funny."

She giggled, reaching for a greenish yellow crayon. "*I* thought so."

Kevin and Gopher continued to hunt for the paper. With so many other papers lying about, it wasn't easy. They were just about to call it quits when Kevin's father walked in.

"Dad!" cheered Kevin. "You're our last hope. Have you seen today's paper?"

"Sure, don't you remember? I used it to cover my head this morning when I picked you up at the pond."

The two boys dashed out to the truck. They found the paper, soggy and torn. Gopher couldn't possibly use it.

"Oh, darn," said Kevin. His mouth went into that peculiar S shape. "Darn, darn, darn." Now that there was no other way for

Gopher to enter the contest, it looked as if Kevin was really struggling: should he give back the picture of Dino-Mighty or not?

"That's okay," said Gopher, trying to help. "You liked the picture so much, that was fun enough for me. I don't care about a dumb contest, anyway."

"You don't care?"

Gopher shrugged. He *did* care, but what could he say? He'd given the picture away. Anyway, he probably wouldn't have won: lots of kids enter these contests.

"Gee, thanks," said Kevin. "*Thanks a million!*"

Kevin must really love it, the way he keeps thanking me over and over, Gopher thought. He could imagine his best friend enjoying looking at Dino-Mighty pinned to his closet door with that bent green thumbtack for months and months. Taking into account how Kevin never threw anything away, maybe even *years!*

The Winner

On a Monday morning two weeks later Mrs. Morrison, Gopher's fifth-grade teacher, stood in front of the class. She had what looked like a newspaper in her hand. "Someone in this class has received a very special honor," she said. She smiled at Kevin. Kevin looked embarrassed. Gopher had no idea what she was talking about. Kevin hadn't mentioned any special honor.

She shuffled through the paper. "Yes, Kevin Gordon entered *The Kids' Page* drawing contest a couple of weeks ago. I saw in Saturday's paper that he'd won." She held up a page. "Here's the picture he drew."

Gopher could hardly believe his eyes. It was Dino-Mighty! He looked at Kevin for an answer. Kevin stared straight ahead.

"It says here that the winner received twenty-five dollars. So, Kevin, you're a rich boy today, aren't you? Isn't that exciting, class?"

Now, Gopher could hardly believe his ears as well as his eyes. Kevin had sent in Dino-Mighty and put his own name on it?

"Boy, you sure are lucky!" said Lance, who sat in the next row.

Mrs. Morrison scowled. "Wait just a minute. Did I hear the work 'lucky'? This isn't like the lottery where one is merely 'lucky.' Kevin worked hard for this prize. He had to make a drawing using these certain lines. Didn't he do a terrific job?"

Gopher's head felt like it was full of soapy water. He wanted to say that it was *his* drawing, but he was so overwhelmed he couldn't speak.

Kevin just kept staring in front of him, as if his desk was on automatic pilot. And he was the automatic part.

Mrs. Morrison, holding the picture, walked around the room. "I'll tape this onto some construction paper and then I'll put it right there on the bulletin board. That way we all can enjoy it for a long time." She took another long look at the picture before putting it away. "That's really an excellent drawing, Kevin. We're extremely proud of you."

Kevin didn't answer, just kept up his automatic pilot act. Finally he picked up his pencil and pretended—so it looked to Gopher—to be engrossed in his work.

Gopher sat there, too stunned to move. He felt sick. He shouldn't let Kevin get away with this! He should speak up! Now! But, he couldn't. He just couldn't.

At recess several kids gathered around Kevin and asked him lots of questions. "How did you know about the contest?" "Where'd you get that neat idea about combining a robot with a dinosaur?" "Do you get to spend the money any way you want?"

Gopher didn't stick around. He didn't want anything more to do with Kevin, his former so-called best friend. He and Kevin had had plenty of arguments before. After all, they'd been friends since second grade when the teacher had sat them in alphabetical order. Since "Goff" came right before "Gordon," Gopher had sat in front of Kevin that whole year. Gopher could hardly remember any of the arguments—what they were about that is—but there had been plenty.

But this was different. This was really sneaky. Gopher would hate him until his dying day.

As for how Kevin was going to spend the money, Gopher was pretty sure he knew. On the way home from school he walked to Mr. Mahoney's store to see if he was right.

"Yep, Kevin stopped in on Saturday and bought Fried Clyde. I've never seen a kid so happy. He said he won some kind of contest in the newspaper. I guess he's a pretty good artist, from the drawing he showed me."

Gopher felt like crying. This wasn't like somebody stealing a bike or a lunch box. Those things didn't "belong" to you, except that you paid money for them. That drawing *belonged* to him. He had made it with his own hands, from an idea out of his own head. He mumbled good-bye.

"Oh, Matt, by the way," Mr. Mahoney called. "I'm sorry, but somebody bought that airbrush you had your eye on. But I'm sure I'll be getting another one someday."

Gopher was afraid if he turned back he might really start crying. "I-it's okay," he stuttered.

All the way home, Gopher saw nothing but the cracks in the sidewalk and the pavement of the streets. He was so engrossed he barely noticed the smell of french fries and hamburgers coming from the exhaust fan of McDonald's as he walked past.

It occurred to him that losing out on

the airbrush—that was like a regular-hamburger kind of pain. And if it had been anybody else but Kevin who had double-crossed him like this, that would have been a double-cheeseburger kind of pain. But for Kevin—*Kevin!*—to do what he did, that was a Big-Mac-with-fries-and-a-large-drink kind of pain. Gopher gulped back tears. It hurt so much.

As he shuffled along, gradually his misery turned to anger. He wasn't going to take this! He'd get back at that sneak-ball Kevin. How? He didn't have the slightest idea. But he'd think of something!

The Perfect Plan

At school the next morning Gopher noticed that Mrs. Morrison had taped Dino-Mighty onto a piece of red construction paper and pinned it to the bulletin board. The red backing showing faintly through the newspaper made the dinosaur-robot look better than ever. Gopher was determined to get back at Kevin. The trouble was, he hadn't thought of a good way to do it—yet.

After Mrs. Morrison called roll, she pointed the picture out again. Maybe he *should* go tell her. But it was so embarrassing. "That's my picture, Mrs. Morrison," he could imagine himself saying. How dumb. Anyway, if he was going to do that, he should have done it yesterday.

He *could* tell his mom and dad, he supposed. But they'd get upset and call the Gordons. Then everybody in the family would know, even Katie.

Anyway, he wanted to get even himself. If somebody else punished Kevin, it just wouldn't feel as good. He had to think of something really nasty. As nasty as what Kevin had done to him.

"Okay, class, please get out your math books. We'll do some more division problems like yesterday." Mrs. Morrison was standing at the front of the class with a piece of pale yellow chalk in her hand.

Gopher reached into his desk and got out his math book. An old homework paper slipped out. As Mrs. Morrison talked, Gopher started doodling in the margins. Soon, without meaning to, he had drawn a picture of Kevin—with daggers sticking into his stomach! Hey, that was an idea: he could brainstorm all the nasty things he could do to Kevin. And then he'd do them!

"Class, please turn to page 118. Who would like to come to the board and show us how to do problem number 1?" They were starting their second week of double-digit long division. Gopher hated it.

Cut off Kevin's eyebrows was the first idea that popped into Gopher's head. That's a weird one, he thought. But remembering you're not supposed to discard any ideas when you brainstorm, he wrote it down.

"Matthew, do you agree with Gary's answer?"

Gopher looked at the board and tried to act like he'd been working on the math problem all along.

"It looks good to me."

"All right, class, now you've been reminded how to do it. Please do every other problem, starting with the second one." Mrs. Morrison sat at her desk, and kids started going up for individual help.

Cut off Kevin's nose Gopher continued his

list. Boy, that was even weirder than the one before.

Mrs. Morrison looked up and their eyes met. He got out a clean piece of paper and wrote his name, the date, and the page number. Then he wrote a 2, the number of the first problem. He checked what Mrs. Morrison was doing. She was involved with another student.

Throw ketchup at his house, he wrote on the original paper.

Gopher covered his paper with his math book. Mrs. Morrison was going around the class. He studied problem 2. He never could remember how many places over to put the first number.

Mrs. Morrison nodded as she saw him copying the problem. She went on to the next kid.

Gopher sneaked the first paper back.

Tell kids at school that he—Gopher tried to think of the most embarrassing thing he could say about Kevin—*wets his pants.*

Put thumbtacks in the Gordons' driveway.

Steal Andy or Randy.

Gopher looked up. Mrs. Morrison was on the other side of the room. She was frowning at him. He studied problem 2 again: 27 into 1,377? How could anybody ever figure *that* out? He noticed Kevin was just putting his pencil down. He'd already finished?

Steal Kevin's math homework.

Steal Kevin's bike.

Steal Kevin's skateboard.

Gopher stopped writing. That was it! He'd steal Fried Clyde! That would hurt Kevin the most. It would serve him right too. After all, he'd bought it with *his* money.

And it wouldn't be hard to do, either. When the newness wore off in a few days, that skateboard would be left lying around Kevin's yard just like all his other toys. Gopher could just go over and take it. *Now* he could concentrate on long division. It was the perfect plan!

Getting Even

Some days later, on a Friday night, Gopher's mother had to work late and his father was out of town. This might be the perfect night to carry out his perfect plan. He rode his bike over to Kevin's. Sure enough, there was Fried Clyde on the front porch.

A glow was coming from the Gordons' kitchen window. They were probably inside eating dinner. Still, their gray Nova wasn't in the driveway.

Gopher got nervous imagining the Gordons driving up while he was carrying away the skateboard. He got even more nervous imagining them coming out the front door. He wondered if he should forget the whole idea, at least for tonight.

Shucks, he thought, disgusted with himself. Why did he always feel like wimping out? This was no big deal. If Kevin was here, he'd just *do* it. Like on Halloween, Kevin always went right up to Mr. Cloxton's house and rang the doorbell. When the old man opened the door, about four vicious dogs would be barking and growling behind him. "Trick or treat," Kevin would say, calm as anything. Gopher only went along to keep Kevin from calling him a wimp-head.

Gopher took a deep breath. "No guts, no glory," he said to himself. Letting out a sigh, he started to sneak up to the house. He knew it would be smarter to walk normally. He'd been to this house hundreds of times. Why would anybody suspect him? Still, his legs remained bent, his head tucked far down in his jacket. He could barely see.

Some thief I'd make, he thought. He'd even forgotten to bring a bag to carry away the loot.

Luckily, he didn't need a bag. The Gordons weren't home. He quickly picked up the skateboard, ran back to his bike, and pedaled for home.

Once he had gone some distance he felt better. Ha! He'd gotten away with it. And wouldn't Kevin be sorry!

A catchy song drifted into his head. It was one his father sang with his barbershop music group.

> *I'm a Yankee-Doodle Dandy,*
> *A Yankee Doodle, do or die. . . .*

Gopher didn't know exactly what a Yankee Doodle was, but it sounded like a guy who's happy-go-lucky, who does daring stuff like taking back a skateboard that some other guy had bought with *your* money, and he wouldn't think anything about it.

> *A real live nephew of my Uncle Sam,*
> *Born on the Fourth of July.*

He couldn't remember how the song went after, so he just tried to whistle the rest. He was never very good at whistling though, so he sang the beginning two more times, and then he was home.

Nobody else was there yet. He decided to take advantage of being alone to practice awhile on Fried Clyde. Even though his own skateboard was pretty good, it wasn't as smooth as this. These wheels just purred. The sound reminded him of Candy, Kevin's cat. She would lie on his lap for half an hour at a time while he stroked her silky fur. That was B.D. Before Dino-Mighty, when he and Kevin were still friends.

He tried an ollie, and a nollie, and a couple of kick flips. Boy, this board was really designed! He went a couple of inches higher than he could with his own board. And there was more control on the landing. This was one fine machine. Well, good! Kevin would miss it all the more.

He performed a few more moves, and then

he began to get uneasy. His mother might come home at any moment. Besides, it was getting dark. Now he had to decide what to do with the skateboard.

He looked around the garage. That wouldn't do. His mom or dad might find it. The only place his parents didn't go regularly was his room. He'd hide it there.

As he scanned his room for a likely spot, the skateboard grew bigger by about a foot. At least it seemed that way. He'd never seen such a huge skateboard in his life! He tried it under his bed. Covered with the bedspread, it was completely out of view. But what about when his mother, Mrs. Dust-Control, came in to vacuum? He'd better choose another place.

The shelves in the back of his closet were the only other possibility. He rearranged some drawing pads and shoved the skateboard there. It showed plainly. He took out his Boston Museum of Science sweatshirt and covered it up with that. It really made a mess of his shelves, but what could he do?

Then he lay down on his bed. He thought about Kevin and Fried Clyde and Dino-Mighty. He felt a little happy: he'd been able to do something to get even with Kevin. Losing that skateboard would drive Kevin up the wall.

He also felt a little sad: he and Kevin weren't friends anymore.

Besides feeling happy and sad, he felt lonely. He needed to talk to someone.

Then he had an idea. He'd call up Kevin! He'd pretend nothing was wrong. He'd let Kevin think he'd forgotten all about Dino-Mighty and that he wanted to be friends again.

That way he could enjoy hearing how upset Kevin was at losing Fried Clyde!

Calling Kevin

Gopher looked at the clock. His mother was usually home by now. He decided to call right away, before she arrived.

He went to his parents' bedroom and dialed the phone. After eight rings he started to hang up. Then Kevin answered. He sounded out of breath.

"Hello?"

Hearing Kevin's so-familiar voice brought Gopher up short. He'd forgotten how normal it was talking to Kevin. He almost felt ashamed for calling.

"Hello?" Kevin asked again. "Is this some kind of joke?"

Kevin was getting mad, he could tell. In fact, Gopher kind of enjoyed it. He decided to talk. "Hello, Kevin. It's me, Gopher." He tried to keep his voice as natural as possible.

There was silence.

Finally Kevin spoke. "We were just coming in the door when the phone was ringing." He laughed a little as if something about that was funny.

"Yeah, I knew you were out." Gopher hit the side of his head. How dumb can you be? Now Kevin would know he had been at his house! And when he found his skateboard missing, he'd suspect *him!*

"Oh, you called before?"

"Yeah," answered Gopher, relieved.

There was another long pause. This wasn't working out as Gopher had expected. Kevin was supposed to be hollering and whining about losing Fried Clyde. *That* would have been fun.

"So," said Kevin, "whatcha doing?"

"Not much." This was true. At that moment, besides speaking on the phone, Gopher was making a tiny hole in his sneaker bigger by poking his finger in it. "Well, I guess I . . . I guess I'll see you around, okay?" He hoped Kevin would let it go at that.

"Huh? What'd you call for?"

"Well . . ." Gopher tried to think. "Ah, ah . . . maybe we could go skateboarding tomorrow." Skateboarding with that slime-ball was about the *last* thing Gopher wanted to do.

"Really? You mean it?"

"If you can't, it's okay. Bye."

"No, wait. I'd like to. I didn't think *you'd* like to. I thought you were still, you know . . . mad."

Gopher *was* mad. He was furious! But he couldn't tell Kevin that, not now that he had phoned pretending to be friends. "Well . . ." he began, and then he couldn't say anything else.

"You want to come over?" suggested Kevin. Gopher noticed that Kevin was asking politely, not just ordering him, like he usually did.

"Nah, I don't think so."

"Mr. Mahoney called," Kevin went on. "Said he'd like us to help him at the store tomorrow. I told him I'd come by myself, but now you come too, okay?"

Hearing Mr. Mahoney's name reminded Gopher of all the happy times he and Kevin had had at his store. The funny thing was, he hadn't thought of them as "happy times" while they were happening. They were just "regular times" then.

But that was B.D. Now those times were over.

"Nah, can't," said Gopher. He'd almost worked the hole in his sneaker big enough to get his whole finger through.

There was another long pause. "Okay," said Kevin. Gopher was just about to say good-bye again when Kevin brought up another subject. "Hey, did you hear that they rescheduled the hot air balloon rides? They're having them again in two weeks. Or maybe three. Ah—wait a minute." Kevin yelled to someone about the date of the hot air balloons. "Three weeks," he reported when he came back on the phone. "Dad said I could have that or a regular birthday party. I said I'd rather have that. Trouble is, it's so expensive I can only have one friend. You wanna come?"

Gopher felt all mixed up. Of course, he wanted to go on a hot air balloon ride. And it made him happy to hear Kevin say he could only invite one friend and that it would be him. But Kevin had been so sneaky and so rotten, and he hadn't even said he was sorry. It was so confusing—liking someone and being mad at him at the same time. "Nah, I can't," he lied. "I got something I have to do."

"Three weeks from now you got something you have to do?" Kevin obviously didn't believe him. "You usually don't know what you're going to do three *minutes* from now."

"Yeah, well . . ."

"You're sure?" Kevin sounded really disappointed. He waited for Gopher to say once more he couldn't go. "Well, I guess I'll have to ask somebody else," he announced sadly.

Ask somebody *else?* Without meaning to, Gopher ripped the hole in his sneaker to about the size of a quarter. Kevin was going to ask somebody else? That showed how loyal *he* was!

"So, are you coming over tomorrow?" Kevin went on. "I'll let you ride Fried Clyde as long as you want. It's the best."

In that dark bedroom, with nobody to see, Gopher nodded. Fried Clyde *was* good. It was also well hidden in the back of his closet, a fact that Kevin would never know. Especially if he, Gopher, played it right. "Okay, I'll come," he said.

"Great!" cheered Kevin. "See you tomorrow."

"Yeah, bye."

"Hey, and maybe Dad can take us to the pond, too. I'll ask him. Bye."

Before Gopher had a chance to say he didn't want to go to the pond, the phone was dead. Well, he'd go see Kevin in the morning. He wondered what that would be like.

Taking His Mind
off Kevin

After Gopher hung up the phone, he realized how hungry he was. *Where was Mom?* It was almost seven-thirty! Then he remembered to check the answering machine in the den. Sure enough, the red light was blinking. There was a message. He pushed the *Play* button.

"Matthew, honey," the recorded voice of his mother said. "The receipts are way off tonight. It looks like I'll be here for a while. There's food in the fridge. Or, you can take some money from the green box and go to McDonald's. But, *take a friend.* Is Kevin around? Call me when you get this message, so I'll know you're okay, okay? Love ya. Bye."

Gopher called his mom and told her that he didn't feel like going out. He'd just stay home.

"Okay, but lock the door. And if anybody comes, *don't* answer it. I'll buy us some ice cream on my way home, okay?"

He went into the kitchen and took some broccoli quiche out of the refrigerator. While that was heating up in the microwave, he chopped up a hunk of lettuce. Then, taking his food with him, he went to watch television.

His mom still wasn't home when he'd finished eating. He went to his room to look at Fried Clyde some more. He turned the skateboard this way and that. It really was a great design. He decided he'd try to copy it. He got out his drawing pad and pencils.

He placed the skateboard on his bed. The bedspread, attractively arranged in folds, made a good background. He lightly sketched the skateboard's general shape. He got off the chair to look more closely at the turtle's jutting jaw. It took his mind off Kevin a little, but not completely. Then he remembered that police officer who had come to the house some time back looking for Jason Bosworth's skateboard. The officer with the red, clean face. The one with the gun and the bullets.

What if he comes again?

Gopher tried to push that thought away, but it kept popping up. It reminded him of one of those red-and-white bobbers, the kind he and Kevin put on their fishing lines when they went—used to go—fishing together. He got up again to study the turtle's glaring eyes. Odd spikes of white radiated from the pupils. Whoever painted this did an awesome job! Then Gopher remembered that the policeman had said there was a skateboard thief in the area.

They'll think I'm the guy who took the other ones, too!

Gopher pushed that irritating bobber back into the dark water. His heart was beating fast as he sketched in the white spikes. They looked evil and scary. He finished drawing the design and was anxious to add the color. With nervous hands he squirted out huge globs of thick paint onto his palette—orange and purple and green and black.

And they think those kids are stealing them for drugs! They might arrest me for being on drugs, too!

With determined brush strokes Gopher slathered the paint onto the thick paper. Suddenly he felt like taking his loaded brush and smearing it all over the design, wiping out the whole thing. He didn't, but he was glad when it was finished.

He tacked the soppy object on the cork-board to dry. Then he poured some paint thinner into a glass jar and started cleaning his brush. An eye-stinging cloud of sadness engulfed him: he and Kevin weren't friends anymore. He wondered if Kevin was sorry about that. It didn't sound like it. Kevin was ready to invite somebody else on the hot air balloon ride one second after he'd said he couldn't go.

He swished the dirty brush around and around and wiped his nose with the back of his hand. Besides, Kevin had Andy and Randy and all those other pets to keep him company. He was probably playing with one of them right now.

At that moment Gopher really wished he had a pet. You don't feel so lonely if you have a pet. You can take a dog for a walk. You can hold a cat in your lap. You'd know at least *somebody* likes you.

"Matthew, I'm home." It was the cheerful voice of his mother calling from downstairs.

"I'll be right down, Mom." He had to hide Fried Clyde. As he was putting it back he noticed a deep scratch, about six inches long, on the shelf. A small stone caught in one of the wheels must have done that! He felt sick. His dad had worked *hours* sanding and painting those shelves so they'd look perfect.

"I couldn't decide between Rocky Road and Cherries Jubilee, so I bought both. Are you coming?"

The lump of sadness inside Gopher was so big he doubted he'd have any room for ice cream. He arranged the Boston Museum of Science sweatshirt over Fried Clyde. "Yeah, Mom," he called miserably, "I'm coming."

Looking for
Fried Clyde

When Gopher arrived at the Gordon house the next morning, the whole family was in a bustle. "That kid!" said Mrs. Gordon. She was looking under some bushes near the side of the house. "He's lost his new skateboard, the one he bought with his prize money."

She picked up some object—it looked like a rusty hammer—and held it out at arm's length. "Kevin!" When Kevin turned in her direction, she shook the hammer angrily. "See this? This is why we never have a decent tool in the house!" Kevin shrugged a little guiltily. Mrs. Gordon muttered something, put the hammer aside, and went back to her searching. Gopher decided he might as well join in.

"We wondered why you didn't enter that contest, Matt," she said after a moment. "*You're* the artist." She looked at Gopher, waiting for an answer. Gopher debated if he should tell her, let her know what a scum her own son was. It was so amazing how everyone was so dumb about this! Did people really believe that Kevin had drawn Dino-Mighty? *Kevin?*

Gopher pretended he didn't hear. What would be the point in answering? In a few minutes he'd go home and never, ever, have anything more to do with that cheater.

"I *know* I left it right here when I got in the car last night," Kevin complained. He was pointing to the exact spot from which Gopher had stolen Fried Clyde.

"If you left it there, it would still be there, wouldn't it, now?" asked Mr. Gordon, a nasty edge to his voice.

"I'm *positive* I left it there," Kevin said

again, more whiny than before. "I think somebody took it."

Gopher walked to the side of the house and started looking behind some trash cans. When he turned around, Katie was right beside him.

"Gopher," she whispered.

"Yeah?" He had no idea why Kevin's pesky little sister would be whispering to him.

"I don't think Kevin really drew that picture of the dinosaur-robot," she announced, still whispering.

This was interesting. "Why not?"

"*He can't draw.*" She gave him a piercing look. "Something fishy's going on."

Gopher continued looking behind the trash can. Somehow, now didn't seem a good time to tell Katie that the picture belonged to him.

"And he's been acting so weird lately," Katie went on. "Weirder than usual, I mean."

"I haven't noticed," Gopher lied.

"Well, anyway," said Katie, "did you know I also won a contest? The Sensational

Spring Sweepstakes. Would you like to see the six-foot rabbit I won?"

Katie wasn't usually this friendly. Gopher said he wouldn't mind. Then he remembered. "Maybe not today," he added.

She frowned. "What's wrong with today?" She was giving him that piercing look again. "Anyway, do you think you could help me paint a reindeer? I'm entering another contest. This one's for saving the world. I saw your picture of Rudolph outside Mr. Swenson's office."

Well, that explained one thing—why Katie was being so friendly. "I suppose I could." It was nice being asked for advice, even if it was only by a third grader.

"Can I come over *today*?"

"I guess so." She sure was determined.

"Okay. I'll go get the entry blank." With that she left and went into the house.

Everybody else kept looking around the yard. Finally Mr. Gordon announced, "Well, I say it's not here. If it were, it would be right in plain view. Kevin wouldn't have put it someplace where nobody could find it."

"Why don't we call the police?" suggested Mrs. Gordon. "It was probably a kid who used it a few minutes and then dumped it. Maybe someone turned it in."

Call the police? Gopher's mouth suddenly went dry. He hadn't counted on this.

In a few minutes a police car pulled up in front of the house. Carrying a clipboard, a husky officer in a slightly-too-tight blue uniform got out of the car. Gopher couldn't believe it. It was the same officer—the one with the red, clean face—who had come to his house a few weeks earlier!

"You reported a skateboard missing?" the officer asked Mr. Gordon, the first person he came to.

Mr. Gordon called Kevin, and the officer asked him a lot of questions. What did the skateboard look like? When did he buy it? How much did he pay? Was there any chance that a friend might have borrowed it without telling him? The officer wrote down all Kevin's answers. Then he shook his head.

"I hate to sound discouraging," he said, "but these things are hardly ever returned. In fact, this is the eleventh skateboard we've had stolen this month. We don't know what's going on. We think it's some teenagers, stealing them to sell. Drugs, maybe."

The officer scanned the area. When he saw Gopher, he seemed to be trying to remember where he'd seen him before. "You didn't have a skateboard stolen recently did you?" he asked.

"No, sir." Gopher thought it best not to go into detail.

The man got in his car and rolled down the window. "You said it was one of those with that monster turtle picture on it?"

Kevin nodded yes, biting his lower lip and blinking.

"Yeah, that's the kind they go for."

The officer drove off and the family just stood there. Then Mr. Gordon walked over

to Kevin and gently put his arm around him. "Oh, Kevin," he said. "I know how you feel. When I was a kid, somebody stole my bike. You know, here I am, an old guy, thirty-five years old, and it *still* hurts."

With that, Kevin's tears got the better of him and spilled down his cheeks. He looked at Gopher and laughed in embarrassment.

"I'll get over it," he said, referring to his crying. "You want to stay? We can go skateboarding." He laughed again, this time for real. "I'm not lucky enough that anybody would steal my *old* skateboard."

You could always count on Kevin's sense of humor. He rubbed away some tears with the back of a hand. "I mean it. We could do that, or maybe we could go on a hike."

For a moment Gopher almost forgot his promise to himself never to have anything more to do with Kevin. He could tell that his best friend—former best friend—was really broken up about losing the skateboard. For a split second Gopher almost understood how it had happened. How Kevin, always careless and never planning ahead, had sent in the picture without really thinking about it. How, after he'd won, he was too embarrassed to admit what he had done.

Gopher *almost* understood. Besides, Kevin had never said he was sorry or tried to make it up to him one little bit. "Nah, I can't," he said. "I have to go home."

"You do?" Kevin, still not completely over his crying, sniffled. "Are you sure you don't want to help Mr. Mahoney this afternoon?"

"Nah, I can't do that either."

Kevin's mouth went into that peculiar S shape. "You don't want to be friends anymore?" he asked, so quietly Gopher could hardly hear.

Gopher didn't answer, except to shrug. He decided he might as well leave. "Well, I'll see you around." Even as he said it, he wasn't sure he'd ever "see" Kevin—the way he used to—again.

Kevin lowered his eyes and wet his lips

several times. It appeared he was trying to say something, but the words wouldn't come out. He looked at Gopher with sad, watery eyes.

"Well, I gotta go," said Gopher. He started to walk away.

Just then he heard Katie's voice. She was coming out of the house, carrying a large piece of paper. "Okay, Gopher," she called, "I'm ready."

Katie Wonders

"Huh?" Kevin looked at Gopher.

Gopher shrugged. "She asked, and I said okay." He thought it was pretty strange himself.

When Gopher and Katie got back to his house, she showed him the poster. "It's called 'Picture a Better World.' I want to draw all kinds of animals having a good time in nature. Reindeers, raccoons, squirrels, and maybe"—she grinned at Gopher—"some gophers, too."

Gopher explained that when he drew something he liked to *see* the actual thing. "If I draw a tree," he told her, "I usually go outside and look at a tree." Since there were no reindeer or raccoons around, they decided to do the next best thing. He took her to the basement where he kept his supply of *Ranger Ricks*. They started paging through them.

When they'd found a whole bunch of animal pictures, they took them up to Gopher's room. "It's best to make a practice picture first," he explained. He went to the back of his closet to get a drawing pad. Oh, oh. He'd forgotten about Fried Clyde. There it was, only partially hidden by his Boston Museum of Science sweatshirt.

He rearranged the sweatshirt. Even so, it was asking too much: no *human's* sweatshirt could completely cover an object as huge as that skateboard. He picked up a drawing pad and walked out of the closet, making sure he closed the door behind him. "Here," he said, as he handed her the pad.

Katie propped up a copy of a *Ranger Rick* and began. After a couple of minutes she had drawn a fairly decent reindeer. Then Gopher gave her the tracing paper.

Now that she was all set up, he left her alone.

When he came back in half an hour, she'd gotten the reindeer in place, as well as two squirrels and a variety of other animals. Gopher wasn't sure, but he assumed the brown fuzzy somethings sticking their heads out of the ground were gophers. "You're doing a good job," he said.

"Thanks, Gopher." She gave him a smile. "Drawing's fun, even though I'm much better at math."

"Not me!"

"You don't like *math?*" She seemed to think that wasn't possible. "I love it." She stopped talking to pay attention to some small detail of her painting. "You know how people say, 'It doesn't take a rocket scientist'? Well, that's what I want to be when I grow up, a rocket scientist."

Gopher almost laughed out loud. And she said *Kevin* was weird?

She went back to drawing. "While you

were gone—I hope you don't mind—I looked around your room."

Gopher immediately thought of Fried Clyde. "You didn't go in the closet, did you?" He tried to keep his voice casual.

"No, I would never be nosy like that. That's rude."

Gopher hadn't realized Katie had something against being nosy. But, if she did, he was glad to hear it.

"All I wanted was to see exactly how you drew Rudolph." She pointed at the Santa Claus picture.

"That's okay," he said. Then he looked around the room himself. Everything was fine until he got to the cork bulletin board. There, right in plain view, was the painting of Fried Clyde! Maybe Katie hadn't noticed it. He hoped so.

But his hope was soon crushed. "I also liked *that* one." She was pointing at the still damp picture. "So you think I should put the raccoons by the lake or by the tree?"

"Oh, *you* have to decide." Gopher let out a breath. Apparently she wasn't going to ask about the painting. "The fun of art is making your own decisions," he added, just to keep her off the track.

"Hmmm. Okay. I think by the lake." She proceeded to draw a furry black-masked animal. "By the way, Gopher, how did you do such a good job of painting Fried Clyde? Did you have a picture?"

He didn't answer. He couldn't answer. If he said he had a picture, she'd ask to see it. If he said he didn't have a picture, then she'd go back to question number one: how did he do such a good job?

"No picture?" she said, supplying her own answer. "So you drew it right from the skateboard?"

"Well, you know . . ." How did this nosy little kid ever sneak her way into his room in the first place? "I saw it lots of times in Mr. Mahoney's store before Kevin bought it."

Now Katie's face was about six inches from the painting. "You got it so exact." She looked at him hard. "You even got those little spikes of white in the eyes. You remembered all that?"

Gopher gave an awkward laugh. "Well, you know, when it comes to art, I have a pretty good memory." He pointed to his head. "As they say, it doesn't take a rocket scientist."

She went back to her own project. "Hmmm." She was nodding, kind of like she knew something and wasn't telling. "I was just wondering."

"Just wondering?" Just wondering *what?* Gopher didn't like the sound of that at all.

A Surprise at Lunch

At school next Monday the kids were all excited about the disappearance of Kevin's skateboard. "I hope they catch the thief soon, Kevin," said Mrs. Morrison. "I'm so sorry."

"Some jerk!" said Brenda. "Thinks he can have whatever he wants."

"Yeah, I *hate* that," said Lance. "Guys who steal are the scum of the earth."

Gopher sneaked a look at Kevin. He caught Kevin sneaking a look at him. Did Kevin suspect anything? Had Katie told him about the picture of Fried Clyde?

"How come Kevin doesn't eat with us anymore?" Robin asked at lunch that day. Until Dino-Mighty, Kevin had been a regular member of Gopher's lunch group. "He's been sitting with Ben and Mark and those guys lately. I don't get it."

"Beats me," said Gopher. Without talking about it, he and Kevin had worked out this way of avoiding each other. He wondered if Robin and the others also noticed that he, Gopher, had been staying in for lunch recess.

As everyone was getting ready to leave, Stephanie stopped next to him. "You're staying in *again?*" Even though she wore braces, her smile could cheer you up more than anybody's. "You stayed in all last week. What's the matter?"

"Nothing . . . much." He gave her a limp smile. She always seemed so tuned in to what he was feeling. It was like she had some kind of Emotion Detector attached to her brain.

"Is much *much?*" She grinned to let him know she was being silly on purpose. She waited for him to say something.

What could he say? That his best friend had stolen the credit for his drawing? To get even he'd stolen his best friend's skateboard? "Sorta much," he answered softly. Then he shrugged to say he couldn't really talk about it.

"Well . . ." She gave him another one of those beautiful bracey smiles. Then she left.

He got out his math book. Since he felt so bad anyway, he might as well do math. Long division, even! He turned to page 167.

"Just a minute, son." It was the new cafeteria lady. A big green sponge in her hand, she wanted to clean the table. He lifted his book. "You're staying in on a beautiful day like this?" She wagged the wet sponge at him. "Not good for your health, you know." She finished wiping the table and went on to the next one. He put his book back down on the damp table and looked at page 167 again.

He got stuck on the very first problem.

Usually when this happened, in the old days, he'd ask Kevin. He couldn't understand it: with Kevin's help, long division problems had been easy. He turned back a few pages to see if he could remember how to do them again.

Then he sensed somebody standing over him. He looked up. It was the cafeteria lady again. "Do you know anybody named . . . ?" She scowled at the penciled printing on a scruffy white envelope. "It looks like *Gopher?* Do you think there's a kid in this school with a name like that?"

The way she said it, Gopher was embarrassed to admit that there was. "That's me," he said.

"Oh." She stared at him. It seemed like she was trying to figure out if there was anything about the way he *looked* that accounted for that unusual nickname. "Well, then, this must be for you. I found it over on that table." She handed him the envelope and went back to her work.

Gopher studied the babyish printing. None of his friends wrote that way. And why would anybody be sending him a letter in the first place? And leaving it on the cafeteria table? Weird.

He held the envelope to see how heavy it was. It felt empty. Somebody who could barely print was sending him an empty envelope?

But maybe it wasn't empty. He ripped it open. Inside, all by itself, was a crinkled five-dollar bill.

Where Did the Money Come From?

Gopher looked at the envelope again. There was no clue as to who it was from. The only person who had any reason to give him money was Kevin.

The bell rang. Lunch recess was over. Knowing the kids would be lining up, Gopher gathered up his books and ran outside. He found Kevin and shoved the envelope toward him. "Did you send me this?"

Kevin scowled. "Huh?"

"You sent this, right?"

Kevin scowled some more. "What is it?"

"*Walk!*" shouted the school aide, opening the doors. The children rushed into the building.

"C'mon, Kevin, quite fooling." Gopher had to scurry to keep up with him. "It's from you, isn't it?"

"What's in it?" Kevin wasn't even curious enough to slow down.

Gopher studied that face that he knew as well as his own. If Kevin was faking, he was doing a good job. Gopher showed him the money.

"Huh?" Kevin grumped. "Where would I get five dollars from?"

Back in class, Gopher couldn't stop thinking about the envelope. He was sure it was from Kevin. Maybe he could trick him into admitting it. He reached in his desk and pulled out a piece of yellow paper with blue lines. "Kevin," he wrote, "you want to come over after school?" He signed the note and sent it on its way.

Kevin opened the note and made that funny S shape with his mouth. "Can't," he wrote on the same piece of paper.

Not much of an answer, thought Gopher.

Below Kevin's writing he wrote, "Why not?"

"I got something to do," Kevin scribbled.

Something to do? They used to tell each other everything.

"Mrs. Morrison," a girl's voice called out. Gopher looked up to see Brenda at the bulletin board, the one where Mrs. Morrison had displayed the newspaper picture of Dino-Mighty. "Did you notice that Kevin's picture is gone?"

"What?" Mrs. Morrison walked quickly to where Brenda was standing. "Well!" Her eyebrows scrunched into a deep frown. "Class, does anybody know anything about this?"

"I was just walking by on my way to the pencil sharpener," Brenda explained, "and I saw that empty spot." She beamed at the teacher. "It sure was good my pencil broke just then, wasn't it, Mrs. Morrison?"

"Yes, thank you, Brenda. You may take your seat now."

"Even though it *is* my favorite pencil, the one Mr. Swenson gave me for reading ten books. Do you think he'll give me another one, since I was the one who saw the picture's missing first?"

Mrs. Morrison said she doubted it and she'd like Brenda to sit down. "Now, class," she went on. "Somebody in this room has taken something that doesn't belong to him or her. I'm sure it was a mistake." She looked up and down the rows waiting, the way teachers do, for somebody to give themself up. Nobody did. She continued, "We must be together many hours every day. That's not pleasant if we can't trust each other, is it?"

Twenty-four children's heads shook from side to side: no, it wasn't pleasant to be with people you couldn't trust.

"Well, then, I expect to have that picture back by the end of the day. We won't make the person identify himself or herself. The person who took it can leave it someplace around the room, and we'll find it." She shot Brenda a meaningful look. "Won't we, Brenda?"

Brenda gave a very-pleased-with-herself nod.

"Please get ready for dismissal," came the announcement over the loudspeaker at the end of the day. Kevin's picture still hadn't turned up. Mrs. Morrison sighed, as if the disappointment was almost too much. "Well, I hope the person who took it will think about it overnight, how they're affecting the atmosphere of our classroom. It would be very nice to see that picture on my desk first thing in the morning."

Gopher glanced around for the picture on his way out. That someone would steal Dino-Mighty was strange, but not as strange as the five dollars. He still thought it was from Kevin. He decided to follow him, but he soon discovered that wasn't going to be easy. Kevin had his bike. Gopher didn't. He doubted he could keep up for long, but he'd give it a shot. From the direction Kevin was riding he knew one thing: he wasn't going home.

"Hi, Gopher," called a girl's voice. It was Katie. She was carrying a big piece of paper.

"I finished my poster. Wanna see?"

"Not now. I'm in a hurry." Then something occurred to him. "Hey, Katie, where's Kevin going?"

"Who knows?" She shrugged to say this was an unsolvable but unimportant problem. "He never tells me anything."

"So you have no idea? I saw him ride his bike toward Main Street."

"Well, actually I *do* know."

Gopher debated if he should stay and listen or make a dash for it while there was still a chance of catching up. He decided to stay. "How do you know? I thought he never tells you anything."

"He doesn't." She was unrolling the poster whether Gopher wanted to see it or not. "Mr. Mahoney left a message on our machine. I always play back all the messages, even if the light isn't blinking."

"You can do that."

"Oh, sure. You just press *Save*, and then press *Play*. You get to hear everything."

Gopher remembered how Katie had said

being nosy was "rude." As if she really minded. Still, if she knew something, he wanted to know, too. "So, where is he?"

"You're sure you don't want to see my poster?" She almost made it sound like she wasn't going to tell him unless he took a look.

"Maybe later, Katie."

"Okay." She started rolling up the paper, not very pleased. "He's at Mr. Mahoney's."

Of course! Kevin himself had mentioned going there last Saturday. Well, that explained the five dollars, for sure.

Gopher didn't need to say good-bye to Katie. She had run into her friend Bethany and was showing *her* the poster.

On the way home he thought about Kevin's pretending it wasn't him who was paying back the money. Typical. He'd pay the money back, but he'd do it secretly, never admitting anything.

Well, at least he was doing *something* to make up. For Kevin, giving away five dollars was a pretty big deal.

When Gopher got home, he sort of wished

he was with Kevin right then, going out on Mr. Mahoney's truck. He missed—he might as well admit it—Kevin. It just wasn't the same. Why did Kevin have to be such a jerk?

He got out his skateboard and went through a few moves. He remembered very well that Fried Clyde was available, just sitting there in the back of his closet, scratching up his shelves. But, there was no way he'd ever use it outside again. Outside? As if you could ever use a skateboard *inside.* And it was only a matter of time before one of his parents discovered it. Somehow, sooner or later, they discovered everything.

But, wait a minute! His parents weren't home. Kevin was occupied with Mr. Mahoney. Gopher put his skateboard back on the wall of the garage. If this idea worked out, in a few minutes his problems with Fried Clyde would be *over!*

Katie, Always Katie

The more Gopher thought about his idea, the more he liked it. He raced up to his room and opened his closet door. As he reached for Fried Clyde, he couldn't help but notice that ugly scratch it had made on the shelf. Luckily, there were no new ones.

He wrapped the skateboard in two paper bags and strapped it onto the back of his bike. Then he took off. He felt great! He could return the skateboard to Kevin's yard, and nobody would ever know he'd had it.

The Gordons' house looked deserted. This was going to be even easier than he'd thought. He got off his bike and started unfastening the strap.

Then, something awful happened: Katie came out of the house! She was with Bethany. She had a piece of chalk in her hand. Gopher started to jump on his bike, but not in time.

"Hi, Gopher."

He stopped. "Is Kevin home?" he asked.

"Nope." Katie was drawing the two bottom squares of a hopscotch design onto the black driveway. "*Now* do you want to see my 'Picture a Better World' poster?"

Gopher scowled. He didn't want to see her poster. He didn't want to see *her.* He just wanted to get rid of the stupid skateboard. Now, he couldn't. Why did *she* always have to be around?

"Sorry, don't have time. I was just riding by. Tell Kevin I was here, okay?"

"Okay." She started writing a big 1 in the lower left square. "Should I tell him about the skateboard?" She pointed the chalk at the package wrapped up with two paper bags.

"That's not a skateboard."

"Oh?" She cocked her head. "What is it?"

Gopher wasn't prepared for this, although he supposed he should have been. This was the same girl who listened to other people's phone messages. (The one who said it was "rude" to be nosy.) "It's just something," he said.

"Gopher, just 'cause I'm in third grade doesn't mean I'm dumb, you know." Now Katie was writing a big 6 on another square. "Of course, it's *something*."

Gopher couldn't think of anything else he might be carrying on the back of his bike in two brown paper bags. A dog? A lawn mower? A lamp?

"Bye, Katie," he said, pedaling away.

When he got home, he put Fried Clyde back in his closet. He'd return that "something" some other time. *Soon,* he hoped.

Back to Normal

At school the next day, after she'd taken the lunch count, Mrs. Morrison turned a sad face toward her class. "I'm afraid nobody has returned Kevin's picture," she said. "I'm very disappointed."

Kevin had his hand in the air. "I don't care if you put it back up, Mrs. Morrison. Everybody had a chance to see it."

"Thank you, Kevin, but that's not the point. I'm counting on the person who took it to return it."

"I *really* don't care," continued Kevin. There was something about the way he said it that was strange, not his usual joking manner. Gopher couldn't figure it out.

At lunch the cafeteria lady delivered another scruffy envelope to Gopher. This one also contained a five-dollar bill, nothing else. Gopher decided he'd try to return Fried Clyde again, as soon as he could.

In the meantime, maybe he and Kevin could start being friends again. "You want to start doing stuff together again?" he asked as they were lining up to go home. He punched Kevin on the arm. "I miss . . ." He didn't want to come right out and say what he really missed. "I miss . . . doing stuff together."

"Okay," said Kevin, like he was happy and embarrassed at the same time.

"Hey, I have an idea. Would you bring Bandy over on Saturday so my mother can see how un-dusty he is? I've started talking about getting a snake. I think I'm wearing her down."

"Okay."

"Will you please say something besides okay?"

Kevin grinned. "Okay."

The only problem was that Gopher wasn't able to return Fried Clyde as he had planned. Every time he had a chance, either his parents were around or somebody was home at the Gordons.

So on Saturday, while Gopher waited for Kevin to show up, Fried Clyde was still in the back of his closet. With most friends that wouldn't have been a problem, but Kevin wasn't most friends. He treated Gopher's room as if it were his own. He would go into Gopher's closet for any reason—or no reason—at all.

Gopher debated what to do. His mother was downstairs in the kitchen. He couldn't hide it in the garage or the basement—she'd see him walk by. Under the bed had been a pretty good place, except for her vacuuming. Well, she wasn't going to vacuum now. He took the skateboard from the closet and pushed it under his bed. He'd just have to remember to put it back when Kevin left, that's all.

Kevin arrived a short time later, carrying the big wooden cage with Bandy in it. He was huffing a little. His hands were sweaty from holding on to the rope strap.

"My, Kevin, that's a heavy load," exclaimed Gopher's mother. She turned off the mixer. "So, I'm finally going to meet this Bandy I've been hearing about!"

When Kevin removed the heavy cover, she wiped her hands on a towel. Gopher stared at her. She was going to *hold* Bandy? She picked up the slim brownish animal. "Aren't you sweet?" She turned to Gopher. "Matthew, I think *we* should have one of these."

Boy, this was going better than Gopher had hoped! His allergic-to-dust mother wanted a pet snake? He swept away a few strands of grass that had fallen out of the messy cage. "This won't happen with the cage I'm getting," he said. "Mr. Mahoney has a glass fish tank I'm gonna buy."

Gopher's mother put the snake back, and Gopher suggested they take Bandy up to his room. "You hold him for as long as you want," Kevin said when they got there. He was trying to be extra nice, Gopher could tell.

Gopher let Bandy twirl himself around his arm. He even felt brave enough to have him climb onto his shoulder. The next thing he knew, Bandy was nosing around the collar of his shirt.

Seeing what Bandy was doing must have given Kevin an idea. He plucked up Bandy, pulled open Gopher's collar, and carelessly dropped the snake down his back. It fell all the way to his belt.

"Kev-vinnnnn!" Gopher gently wriggled open the bottom of his shirt and removed Bandy. Thank goodness, he seemed to be okay. "Let's put him back now." Gopher didn't mind having the snake down his back, but he sure didn't want to take a chance on hurting him.

Then Kevin lay on the floor with his hands under his head. Gopher lay on the bed beside him. "Do you think Mr. Mahoney still has that fish tank?" Gopher asked. It occurred to him he hadn't been to Mr. Mahoney's for quite a few days.

"You want to go check?"

"Yeah, let's," said Gopher. "If I buy it right now, Mom won't be able to change her mind."

Kevin agreed, and the two boys set out.

"I still didn't ask another friend for the hot air balloon ride," said Kevin as they walked along. "You want to go, or are you still 'busy'?"

"Sure, I'll go," said Gopher, a little embarrassed: Kevin had known all along he was lying. "It's next week, right?"

"Right. *If* it doesn't rain."

When they got to the store, they looked around for a while. Then Gopher used the money in his account to pay for the fish tank. Now they had to carry the bulky object home. It was not a fun job.

Halfway there, they sat down to rest. They were both huffing. "I'm sure we can find another snake just like Bandy," Kevin said. "We'll start the search as soon as we get home, okay?" Then he looked at his hands. They were lined with red marks caused by holding on to the sharp edges of the glass tank. "Instead of Band-*y*, we should call this one Band-*age*."

Good old Kevin, always ready with a joke. Always ready to help. Who else would carry a glass fish tank all these blocks? Who else, especially if he was hot and tired, would help him find a pet snake? Gopher knew the answer: nobody. And after they were done looking for a snake, they'd find other stuff to do. Maybe go skateboarding. Or play some games. Eat junk food. Bother Katie.

He glanced at his friend's sweaty face. Then he readjusted his hold on the fish tank. "Let's go."

Kevin groaned. "Okay, slave driver."

Gopher was *so glad* everything was back to normal.

Under the Bed

When they got home, the first thing they did was go upstairs to get Bandy. "Oh, no," wailed Kevin, looking into the empty cage. "This guy's gotten out about a hundred times!"

"Don't worry," said Gopher with real concern. "He couldn't have gone far."

Both boys got busy looking. Kevin was halfway under the bed before Gopher realized what he was doing. "Wait a minute, Kevin, *I'll* look—"

But it was too late. A second later Kevin appeared from under the bed. Fried Clyde was in his hands.

"So, you're the one!" His voice was hollow. "You're the one!" Tears were welling up. "You pretend . . . to be my friend . . . but

you . . . steal!" The words came out in short painful gasps.

"Yeah? Well, you steal, too! Who was it that stole my picture and sent it in to the newspaper, huh?"

"You *gave* me that picture, remember?" Kevin's eyes narrowed to thin slits. "There's a difference between somebody giving you something and somebody taking it without permission. See, stupid?"

Gopher was so furious he couldn't think of an answer. How could Kevin say writing his own name on Dino-Mighty wasn't stealing? That was the worst kind of stealing! "Just go home," he shouted. "I don't want you for a friend ever again!"

"I'm not going till I find my snake!"

Without further talking both boys again began the search for Bandy. In a few moments Gopher found him under the bookshelf.

"Here, take your dumb snake and your dumb cage."

"Yeah? And what about my skateboard?"

"What about it?" jeered Gopher. "It stays here." He had been willing, *eager*, to give Kevin back the skateboard before. Not now. Not after Kevin accused him of stealing. And wouldn't even admit he'd stolen, too.

"Well, if that's the kind of snot you're gonna be." Kevin was now on his way down the stairs, bumping the cage on each step. "But don't think you're gonna get away with this. I'm gonna call the police. Then you're gonna be in *big* trouble!"

Kevin had to walk through the kitchen on his way out. "Bye, Mrs. Goff," he muttered. He slammed the door with a loud bang.

From his bedroom window Gopher watched him go. Kevin must have suspected he'd do that, because he turned and looked at him. He made an ugly face and shook his fist. Gopher answered by sticking out his tongue.

What Does Stephanie Think?

Gopher felt pretty lousy after that. He could tell his mother noticed, because she was extra cheerful. "Dad and I are going out tonight," she reminded him. "Why don't you invite Kevin and a couple of friends over for pizza?"

Gopher didn't feel like having friends over. He certainly didn't want Kevin! He told his mom he'd be okay by himself.

After he'd had dinner, he went to his room. He got out his drawing pad, but somehow that only made him feel worse. Holding his thick drawing pencil, he realized it was the drawing of Dino-Mighty that had started all this. All these *conclusions* from one stupid picture! No wonder he wasn't in the mood to draw.

Maybe if he talked to somebody he'd feel better. He thought of Kevin. Of course, he couldn't call *him.* Then he thought of Stephanie and her Emotion Detector. She'd probably have something helpful to say. But he couldn't call her. Not at nine o'clock on a Saturday night. Or could he?

He decided to do it. He'd called her before, he could call her now. But what would his excuse be this time?

He got out his book bag and went through the homework due for Monday. There was a page of math problems, his usual source of excuses. But these were so easy even *he* hadn't had trouble. Still, if he didn't find anything better, he could pretend to be stuck. Stephanie would just think he was a little dumber than he really was.

And then there was the writing assignment: "Write about a time in your life when you learned something." Gopher had already finished. He'd written about the time Fletcher Simpson had been stealing his milk money. He'd learned something then, all right. Even so, it would be interesting to find out what Stephanie was writing about. He dialed her number.

"Oh, hi, Gopher." Stephanie didn't *sound* like she thought it was strange getting a call from him at nine o'clock on a Saturday night. "Whatcha doing?"

"Nothing much." Then silence. Hearing Stephanie's voice, he got so rattled he couldn't remember his excuse for calling.

"Just felt like talking?" she asked.

Although that was the exact truth, it was a little embarrassing to say so. Next time he'd *write down* how he planned to begin. "Yeah, I guess so," he admitted.

"I get like that lots of times, especially when I'm in the house by myself at night."

Gopher could tell her Emotion Detector was working extra well tonight.

There was another silence. Gopher's mind was a complete blank. There must be *something* they could talk about. Then— he couldn't believe it—he heard himself say, "Isn't that awful how somebody stole Kevin's skateboard?"

"Oh, I know!" She sounded devastated, like her cat had been run over by a car or something. "Some *creep!*"

Gopher cringed. He didn't like being called a creep. Especially by Stephanie.

"Just imagine," she went on, "he saved up for almost a year. And then some *jerk*, just on a whim, probably, stole it!"

Being called a jerk was even worse. Gopher tried to think of something else to talk about. Then, thank goodness, he finally remembered his excuse. "What are you doing for writing?" he asked. "You know, something that taught you something?"

"Actually, it's a little funny, but it's something that has to do with Fletcher Simpson."

"With Fletcher?" That's what he, Gopher, had written about!

"Yes. Remember the time Fletcher thought I stole his three dollars? How he grabbed the money out of my pencil box and was holding on to it? And I reached over and took it out of his hand? I was never so scared in my whole life."

Gopher remembered. "You sure didn't look scared. I thought you were terrific!"

"Thanks, Gopher, but don't go by how people *look*. I was really scared."

Now that Stephanie had told him what she'd written about, Gopher decided to bring up the real reason he'd called. "Speaking of stealing"—he cleared his throat—"what would you do if somebody stole something from you? I mean, not exactly *stole*, but, you know, took credit for something you made?"

Stephanie said she didn't understand.

"Like, say you wrote a poem, and then the other person took it and said it was their poem?"

"Well," said Stephanie, "I'd probably tell the person that I knew what they did. And then if they changed and gave the poem back, I'd probably just forget about it."

"But say the person *didn't* change, he just kept the poem and wouldn't say it was yours?"

"Hmmmm, that's hard. It sounds like bragging to go say, 'I did it.' And then the other person says, 'I did it,' and it goes on like that."

"Yeah, I know," said Gopher. "I can't figure that out either."

Neither one spoke for a moment. "And what are you writing about, Gopher?" Stephanie obviously thought he was done talking about his problem, but he wasn't.

"What do you think about getting even? You know, stealing something from them?"

"Is that what you're writing about? Stealing something?" Stephanie sounded a little surprised.

"No, no," Gopher answered quickly. He didn't want to put ideas like that in her head. "I was still talking about when somebody steals something from you, like a poem. What about getting even by stealing something back?"

"Probably wouldn't work. What are the chances that they'd have something to steal? Anyway, why would anybody steal a poem?"

"Maybe 'cause yours was better?"

"Hmmmm." Gopher liked that Stephanie was taking his question so seriously. "Gee, Gopher, I don't know."

"Well, it doesn't matter." He tried to sound like it wasn't anything. "Well, I guess I'd better go."

"Okay, but you never told me what you're writing about."

"It's kind of funny. I'm writing about Fletcher, too." He chuckled so she would think he was making a joke. "Do you think he's writing about us?"

"Gee, Gopher." She made it sound like a compliment. "You ask the silliest questions."

Getting Rid of
Fried Clyde

Gopher hung up the phone. Stephanie sure hadn't given him a straight answer. He'd sort of hoped she might. But then, why should she? She was just a kid too. And, besides, he hadn't really told her anything. She probably thought he was just talking about some *imaginary* problem.

Then he remembered she'd said she'd "just forget about it." The more he thought about that suggestion, the better he liked it. And the first step was to return that stupid skateboard, once and for all.

He wrapped Fried Clyde in two large paper bags, just as he'd done before, that time he'd run into Katie playing hopscotch in the drive-way. Now, this late at night, he hoped that pesky third grader had the sense to be inside, where she belonged. He strapped the skateboard onto his bike and set off.

As he pedaled along he thought that he'd never seen the roads so dark and spooky before. There's nothing here in the night that isn't here in the day, he told himself. So why should he be scared? There was no reason. But it sure was dark and spooky.

When he got to Kevin's house, the lights were on. There were even a couple of cars in the driveway. He guessed the Gordons were having company. He parked his bike behind some bushes and started removing the paper bags. He'd never noticed before that ordinary paper bags made such a racket.

When he finally had the skateboard free, he looked around. Luckily, no one—at least, no one he could see—had heard. Slouching toward the house, he carefully placed Fried Clyde on the front porch.

Then he remembered the skateboard thieves. Eleven skateboards stolen in a

month, the tight-blue-uniformed police officer had said. He'd better ring the bell so
someone would come and take the darned
thing inside. He pushed the bell, one long
ring, and dashed behind the bushes.

After a few seconds Mr. Gordon opened
the door and looked out. "Who's there?" He
shielded his eyes with his hand. "Marion,
didn't you hear the doorbell ring a second
ago?" he called back into the house.

Gopher couldn't hear what Kevin's
mother answered, but a second later she
too was at the door. Neither one glanced
down at the porch floor where the skateboard was lying. Gopher thought that
would be the first place you'd look if you
were wondering who had rung the doorbell.
But Mr. and Mrs. Gordon just kept staring
into the distance.

Gopher got a little nervous that they
might come outside and start looking
around. Then he'd be a goner. How in the
world would he explain his presence behind
their bushes at this time of night?

"Maybe it was a fluke in the electricity," said Mrs. Gordon. She turned to go back into the house. "Let's not worry about it."

They went back in, and the skateboard stayed right where it was. Gopher didn't dare go back and ring the bell again. He'd just have to leave the thing there . . . and hope that Kevin would find it in the morning.

He rode back through the eerie darkness in silence. He imagined what Kevin would say if he was there. He'd have some wisecrack about "un-stealing" other people's skateboards. He'd be making howling noises to make the scary night even scarier. He'd be laughing and saying how dumb can you be, not looking down at the porch?

As it was, Gopher peddled home by himself, as fast and as hard as he could. He couldn't wait to be in his own house again.

One for the Records

The next morning was Sunday, so Gopher and his parents went to church as usual. When they got home, Kevin was sitting on the back steps. He held up a hand in a sort of wave.

"Kevin!" said Gopher's mother. "Can you stay for breakfast? I'll be making scrambled eggs . . . bagels . . . cantaloupe." She was working the key in the door.

"Thanks, Mrs. Goff, but I don't think so. I'll just be here with Gopher for a couple of minutes. Then I have to go home."

"You'll be missing a great breakfast," added Gopher's father.

"Thanks anyway."

Gopher's mom made a little frown. Then

she and Gopher's father went into the house.

"I've been thinking," said Kevin as soon as they were by themselves. "I shouldn't have sent in your picture. And I wish I didn't. And I wish we were still friends." It sounded like he had memorized what he wanted to say.

Kevin's speech caught Gopher off guard. He had hoped he would never have to think about that stupid Dino-Mighty again. "Yeah, you're right," he answered. "You shouldn't have sent it in." He didn't mean it in an angry way. Kevin had said he shouldn't have done it, and to Gopher that made sense.

"Well, like I said, I'm sorry." Kevin spoke softly, not looking at Gopher.

"Yeah," answered Gopher. "Let's forget the whole thing."

Kevin didn't seem to hear. "It's just when you said you weren't going to send it in, I thought this good chance to make twenty-five dollars was going to waste."

"It's okay, it's over."

"So I sent it in myself. I didn't think you'd mind *so* much."

"It's okay, really." Gopher could see how sad Kevin was. "Really."

Kevin gave a small smile as he picked up a stick and started poking holes in the dirt. "Why don't you just keep the skateboard? It belongs more to you than to me, anyway."

Gopher frowned. Why would Kevin be joking at a time like this? "Keep it? How can I keep it when I left it on your front porch last night?"

"You did?"

"Didn't you hear the doorbell? Your parents came out."

"It was *you* who rang the doorbell?" Kevin scratched his head and smiled. "I'm glad my dad doesn't know."

"Well, did you look on the front porch this morning? It's probably still there." Gopher was getting nervous.

"No, I came out the other way. Why don't

we go back and get it. When they ask us where we found it, we'll say in the woods."

Gopher called to his mom that he was going to Kevin's house. "Kevin, you'll change your mind and have breakfast with us, won't you?" she called back.

"Sure."

As they walked up to the Gordons' front porch, Gopher's sinking feeling got worse. The skateboard wasn't there. How were they going to keep to their story about finding it in the woods if someone in the family had found it first?

They went in the house. The only person around was Katie, sprawled on the living room floor. She was reading the Sunday comics.

"Katie, did you find something on the front porch this morning?" Kevin asked.

"Yes." She gave her big brother a tight smile. "I found something." She said it teasingly, as if she knew Kevin was playing a joke. Gopher couldn't see what was so funny.

"Well, can I have it?" said Kevin. "Please?"

Katie grinned. "Say, 'pretty please.'"

"Katie!"

"O-kay, o-kay." She took part of the comics and held them out in Kevin's direction. "Here, you can have half."

"Comics?" Kevin was speechless. "Who wants the *comics*? I want the thing you found on the front porch!"

"And that's what I'm giving you." She said it extra clearly, as if she was talking to someone who wasn't very smart.

The two boys rolled their eyes and went outside.

"Let's look around the yard," said Gopher. "Maybe it slid off the porch into the bushes." He didn't really believe it, but he and Kevin began the search anyway. The skateboard was nowhere to be found.

"This time it's really gone," groaned Kevin. "That's something for *The Guinness Book of World Records* . . . having the same skateboard stolen from the same place twice."

Gopher knew if he didn't say what was on his mind right then he'd never say it. "Kevin?"

"Yeah?"

"I'm sorry."

Kevin shrugged. "It doesn't matter." His mouth was in that S shape. He gulped once, and then again.

Gopher wished he could go and hug Kevin, actually put his arms around him.

But he and Kevin didn't do stuff like that. So he just stood there sending out good thoughts. He hoped his friend since second grade was getting some of them.

Suddenly those good thoughts were interrupted. "Kevin!" It was Katie. She was standing at the front door. "You'd better come and find Bandy. He's gone again."

In Katie's Closet

Kevin, with Gopher right behind, bounded into the house. "That's the *thousandth time!*" he yelled. "He just won't stay in his cage."

The two boys began the hunt. It took only a few minutes to find Bandy curled up in Kevin's blue jeans, comfortable as you please. Kevin opened the shoddily made cage. Then he stopped. "Gopher, if I put him back, he's just gonna get out again." He handed the snake to Gopher. "Here, you take him home. You have a *nice* cage."

"Gee." Bandy squeezed Gopher's hand and gave him a great big smile. At least that's how it seemed to Gopher. "Thanks!"

"No problem." Kevin reached for a shoe

box and dumped the contents onto the floor. "You can carry him home in this."

Gopher took a pencil and punched a couple of holes in the box. Wow! How lucky can you be?—Bandy was going to be *his*!

Then Kevin looked thoughtfully at Gopher. "I think there's something else I should give you, or at least show you." He surveyed his messy room. "It might take me a couple of minutes to find it, though."

Gopher said Kevin didn't have to give him anything, and why didn't they just take Bandy home and have breakfast.

"No, it's *yours*, and I'm going to find it."

Gopher knew what these searches were like—he'd wait in the living room. Katie was there, still engrossed in the comics.

"So, Katie?" He figured he might as well talk to Kevin's little sister, just to be polite. "Did you win the 'Picture a Better World' poster contest or not?"

"Don't know yet. Maybe." She looked up. "Hey, you never saw the big rabbit I won for the Sensational Spring Sweepstakes. C'mon, I'll show you."

Katie led him to her room, which was a duplicate, messiness-wise, of her brother's. She pointed to a six-foot pink rabbit propped up in the corner. "Isn't he beautiful! I call him Mr. Rabbit." She put her arms around the huge stuffed animal and rubbed her face against its soft pink fur.

Actually, Gopher thought the rabbit was one of the ugliest things he'd ever seen, but he could sort of understand why *Katie* would like it.

"Who knows?" She was still hugging the big fat object. "Maybe someday I'll paint a picture of it." She gave Gopher a two-eyed wink. "The way you painted a picture of Fried Clyde."

"Huh?"

She left the rabbit and opened her closet door. "Here, look." There wasn't much to see except piles of clothes. She dug away at the biggest one, and—Gopher couldn't believe it!—*There was Fried Clyde!*

"When I went out to get the paper this morning, it was right on the porch."

"You found it? And you didn't tell Kevin?" Boy, sisters sure could be nasty to their brothers. "Why?"

Katie shrugged. "I didn't have anything to give him for his birthday." Then she pointed reluctantly to the six-foot stuffed toy. "Although, I suppose I *could* give him Mr. Rabbit."

Gopher regarded the stupid-looking rabbit once more. What in the world would a fifth-grade boy want with a monstrosity like that? "I think Kevin would rather have Fried Clyde," he said.

"You really think so?" Katie seemed relieved. "I want to give him something really *good*. He's been pretty nice lately."

For a second Gopher wasn't sure if she was talking about her brother or Mr. Rabbit. He'd never heard her say anything nice about Kevin before.

"Dad said he could invite two friends to go on the hot air balloon ride." She made a proud face. "He invited *me*."

"He did?" Gopher was having trouble getting all this stuff into his head. Fried Clyde wasn't stolen? And Kevin had invited his little sister?

"Tell me something." He was still curious about her Fried Clyde comment and that two-eyed wink. "Did you know where that skateboard was, *before*?"

"You must have had it." She was removing the frilly pink ribbon from the huge rabbit's neck. "Otherwise, how could you have painted it so perfectly?"

"You knew? And you didn't tell Kevin?"

"Nah. I figured he probably took your drawing and that's why you took his skateboard. He had it coming. Here, put your finger there." She indicated that she wanted Gopher to hold the ribbon, which she was now tying around Fried Clyde. "Anyway, I knew you'd return it as soon as you got done being mad at him. That's what you were trying to do when you came over on your bike, wasn't it?"

This was amazing. "I think you might be a rocket scientist after all," he said, really meaning it.

"Actually, I'm thinking of being an artist instead." She lifted up the beribboned Fried Clyde for him to see. "What do you think?"

That girly pink ribbon wrapped around the monster skateboard looked a little— odd. On the other hand, it made it the perfect gift—for Katie to give to Kevin. "He'll like it," he said with certainty.

Katie put the skateboard back in the closet. "I'll give it to him at lunchtime. Then Mom and Dad can be there, too."

"Gopher!" Kevin was calling. "I found it."

"Well, I gotta go."

"Okay, but please don't tell Kevin." She giggled. "I want to surprise him myself."

"Ballooning Buddies"

When Gopher reentered Kevin's room, he noticed Kevin was holding a couple of pieces of paper. One was a ragged section of newspaper, an article or an advertisement obviously ripped out by hand. The other was a piece of red construction paper with something attached to it. Gopher stared. It was the newspaper picture of Dino-Mighty! The one Mrs. Morrison had put up on the bulletin board. The one Brenda had discovered missing. *Kevin* had stolen it?

Kevin handed the picture to Gopher. The space where Kevin's name had been written was blacked out. Above it, in Kevin's handwriting, were the words "Matthew Goff."

"Aw, Kevin." Gopher didn't want the picture. He didn't want anything that would remind him of all that lying and cheating.

"I'm not *giving* this to you," Kevin said. "I'm only *showing* it to you. You think I can take Mrs. Morrison telling us how disappointed she is in us forever? On Monday, I'm going to give it back to her. But I'm going to give it back with *your* name on it. Do you think she'll notice?"

Gopher didn't see how Kevin could be serious. "How could she not notice?" He couldn't keep from smiling.

"Well, if she does, I guess I'll have to explain the whole thing." Kevin's mouth went into that peculiar S shape. He scratched his head. "You really think she'll notice?"

Gopher laughed out loud. "Of course, she'll notice!" He pointed to the part where Kevin's name had been blacked out. "How dumb would you have to be not to notice that?"

"Hmmm." Kevin grinned. "Pretty dumb, I

guess." He let out a big breath. "And I'm sure when she puts it back up, all the kids would notice, too?"

"Well, at least Brenda." Gopher knew what was going through Kevin's mind. He sort of enjoyed it.

Kevin's mouth took another couple of S turns. "Well, anyway, I'm gonna do it. So what if all the kids think I'm a punk and a thief?" A strange look passed over his face. "I *am* a punk and a thief!"

Gopher took the picture and pretended to study it carefully. Then, before Kevin could stop him, he ripped it in two. Next he ripped the twos into fours, the fours into eights. He kept this up until the picture and its red backing looked like so much giant confetti. "Wheeee!" He flung the pieces into the air.

"Now look what you've done," Kevin cried out in mock horror. "What's Mrs. Morrison going to think?"

"She'll get over it." Gopher bent down to pick up the pieces, but then he decided not to. He'd leave the mess right there, just like Kevin would. "It wasn't exactly the *Mona Lisa*, you know."

Kevin frowned as if he wasn't sure what Gopher meant. "Well, I might as well tell you about something else while I'm at it. You know those envelopes in the cafeteria? They're from me."

"*No!*"

"Yeah, I worked for Mr. Mahoney. Since I was doing it by myself, he gave me half on account and half in cash. That's where I got the money from."

"I figured that out a long time ago," said Gopher. "The only part I didn't know was that you had such bad handwriting."

Kevin laughed what sounded almost like his old laugh. "Well, I had to use a *disguise*. I wrote them with my left hand."

"I thought you wrote them with your left *foot.*"

Kevin laughed some more. "Anyway, I'll keep paying you back until you get all the money."

If Kevin was going to keep paying him back, then they still wouldn't be over it. "No, Kevin, don't do that. I don't want any money."

"Really?"

"Really."

Kevin shrugged. "Well, then I guess you better get ready to work. Mr. Mahoney has another load for us next Tuesday." He socked Gopher on the arm. "And I'm getting tired of doing your share."

Gopher nodded. This was the way he liked it. "Aren't you starving?" He was thinking of his mother's breakfast waiting for them at home.

"Yeah, but I didn't have a chance to show you this." Kevin pushed the ragged-edged piece of newspaper toward Gopher. It was an advertisement for the hot air balloon show. Displayed were a bunch of T-shirts, all with pictures of hot air balloons on them. "See, this guy uses an airbrush to make any design you want. I like this one."

He pointed to a T-shirt that featured a man and a woman flying in a hot air balloon. On the basket part it said "Dan and Heather."

"What a great idea!" said Gopher. "Let's each get one. It will show us two, and yours will say, 'Gopher and Kevin' and mine will say, 'Kevin and Gopher.' What do you think?"

"I like it. And on this part"—Kevin was indicating the balloon portion now—"let's have the guy write, 'Ballooning Buddies.'"

Gopher thought about it. He liked the way it sounded, but "Ballooning Buddies" only captured one small aspect of their friendship.

It didn't include that it was mainly Kevin he wanted to talk to when something especially bad, or good, happened.

It didn't include how much fun it was to be together, even when there was nothing to do.

It didn't include—getting over Dino-Mighty.

But still, Gopher decided, you couldn't expect to tell all there was about such a good friendship on the front of a T-shirt.

"Well?" asked Kevin, still waiting for an answer.

Gopher picked up a handful of the giant confetti and jammed it down the back of Kevin's shirt. "It's dynamite!" he hollered. Then he started running, before Kevin could get him back.

About the Author

Virginia Scribner admits that her son, the "real" Gopher, was never good at art. "It was his friend who won the art contest," she says. "My son was good at math, just the opposite of the book." The part that *is* the same, she adds, is that best friends have fights—and those are the kind that hurts the most.

Ms. Scribner's first book was *Gopher Takes Heart,* which *Booklist* called "entertaining and believable." She is presently at work on a third book about Gopher.

The author, a school librarian, lives in Rhode Island with her husband. They have three grown children.